Jane Knight worked for several years at an Oxfordshire school for children with severe learning difficulties. During this time, she studied art history and literature with the Open University, gaining an honours degree. She went on to study Clinical Communication at City University, London, qualifying as a Speech and Language Therapist.

Jane has always been fascinated with the idea of guardian angels, so when she had the idea of writing a story for her grandchildren, it naturally evolved with this theme.

She believes kittens and angels are a perfect combination for any child to love.

Kitty Angel

Jane Daphne Knight

AUSTIN MACAULEY PUBLISHERS™

LONDON • CAMBRIDGE • NEW YORK • SHARJAH

A CIP catalogue record for this title is available from the British Library.

ISBN 9781788783620 (Paperback)
ISBN 9781788783637 (Hardback)
ISBN 9781528955447 (ePub e-book)

www.austinmacauley.com

First Published (2019)
Austin Macauley Publishers Ltd.
25 Canada Square
Canary Wharf
London
E14 5LQ

For my grandchildren, Will and Katie, whose wild enthusiasm for each chapter of *Kitty Angel* kept me writing. Jack and Harry, who always make me laugh with their crazy boy fun.

My husband, David, who encouraged me to publish my story and always gave me great advice! My son, Simon; daughter, Rachel; and daughter-in-law, Leanne, for their enthusiasm and interest.

'The Illustration of Kitty Angel is based on original drawings by David Knight'

Chapter One

Will and Katie lived with their mum in a small market town where most people knew each other. Their neighbours were kind and helpful, if a little on the nosey side. Their home was a lovely little Victorian terraced house, it was a two up, two down, with just a tiny yard at the back; a big change from the house they had when Dad was around. Mum said they would get used to it, but they'd been there now for over six months and it was still hard, very hard; particularly as Will and Katie now had to share a bedroom.

Yuck was what Katie thought of this arrangement when Mum explained that she wouldn't have a room of her own, fancy having to share a bedroom with your stinky big brother, that's gross.

Will's feelings on the matter are completely unprintable!

The kids didn't like to make a fuss as Mum was already upset quite a lot these days; they tried hard to be good, they really, really did, but somehow, they just seemed to be very good at being bad!

Will and Katie didn't understand why Dad had gone away; they didn't understand about redundancy and how it had made Dad feel like a failure; they didn't understand how low his mood had become and that he felt sure they would be much better off without him. What they did understand was that they woke up one morning and Dad didn't come in to wake them up as he usually did, he wasn't there to make the toast as he usually did and he wasn't there to give them a hug and ruffle their hair before they went off to school as he usually did.

Mum never wanted to talk about their situation, she would just say, "You're far too young to understand."

But it was worse not knowing, and they often wondered if they had done something bad, very bad, and that's why Dad had gone away.

The kids had no real idea about what was going on, and Mum didn't quite know how to explain why Dad had left them, she wasn't sure herself how it had all come about, and so it was easier just to say nothing.

Anyway, here they were in a tiny little house, in a fairly run down part of the town, a long way from the leafy suburbs where they lived before.

Katie and Will felt sad and confused. It's hard when you're only nine and eleven years old to really be able to understand adults and their 'funny ways'! What the kids were both in agreement with was that they needed something to bring a bit of joy into their lives, a bit of happiness after these recent sad months. They both had the same idea, the only thing that would really give them back their smiles was a KITTEN! A cute, white, cuddly kitten; all soft and fluffy!

The big problem was convincing Mum that this was the best idea in the whole, entire, wide world.

The kids made a plan. The plan was that they would be so good, so helpful, so kind and never ever complain, always do their homework, always tidy their room, always fold and put away their clothes and hardest of all, always eat their vegetables!

Unfortunately, they weren't very good at all with keeping to the 'plan', it was all far too much like hard work, and lots of things got in the way, like playing with friends, watching TV, riding their bikes, swimming, going to gymnastics, going to Triathlon club, downloading from iTunes, playing on the Wii, composing songs on the keyboard and generally lounging around!

They decided that they needed another plan; this new plan consisted entirely of begging and pleading with Mum. The conversation went something like this:

"Please, Mum, can we have a kitten? We promise to look after it, play with it, feed it and clear out the litter tray."

"No," said Mum, "kittens make too much mess, cost too much money to feed, leave hair all over the furniture and wee on the carpet."

Not a good start, thought Katie and Will.

"But Mum, kittens are so cuddly and soft and cute and they make everything feel better," said Katie.

"If only that were true," muttered Mum. "No, this house is just too small and all my money goes on you two already," she added.

"We'll do lots more jobs, and you won't know the kitten's here; it will be so good and quiet and clean and not leave hair anywhere and oh, perfect!" cried Will.

But Mum wouldn't budge, she just couldn't see how much it meant to the children; really she was just worn out with working and trying to make ends meet!

Chapter Two

Half-term was coming up and they were going to stay with their cousins, Jack and Harry. They loved spending days with the boys and always had a great time. Jack was three years old, he had big, blue eyes, was bubbling with personality and really cute and hilarious; while Harry was still a baby, a really smiley, gorgeous, wriggly baby who never seemed to cry!

The children all loved each other very much.

They would have so much fun that surely all thoughts of kittens, even cute, white, soft, cuddly ones, would be pushed to the back of their minds.

Friday night arrived and they had the terrible, enormous, almost impossible job of packing up their clothes, toys and bits and bobs in preparation for heading to Uncle Simon and Auntie Leanne's.

Katie had to take so many things with her, it was unbelievable!

"Just in case," she kept muttering.

Just in case!!! thought Will. *Just in case what? Just in case we might end up staying at Uncle Simon and Aunty Leanne's for the rest of our complete, utter and entire lives???*

Will just didn't understand girls. *Never could and never would, that's for sure!* he thought to himself.

After Mum had done lots of nagging and also done lots of repacking, at last the job was done and the kids were bundled into the car for the short journey.

There was high excitement when they arrived. Jack was jumping up and down with glee, and Harry was bouncing up and down in Uncle Simon's arms with a huge grin on his face!

This was going to be so much fun, all the kids were thinking. They were all sure in their own way that the four of them could easily outwit the adults; which meant getting up to all sorts of fun and games!

They had no idea that this was a week when magic would surround them in so many ways.

A week when something very special would be working its way into Will and Katie's world!

It was not just going to be a week of fun, but a week of mystical, mysterious wonders!

During the following week, some amazing things happened:

First of all, they saw a fantastic, beautiful, brilliantly coloured rainbow; it was spectacular and almost otherworldly!

"Make a wish!" cried Will.

So the children all held hands, even Harry, and they closed their eyes and made a wish. Will and Katie wished for, well, I'm sure you can guess; yes, of course, a little white, cute and cuddly kitten. Jack wished for a shiny red bike and a shiny yellow tractor and a shiny green digger and a whole lot more, but, well, he was only three after all! And Harry, well, Harry made a small baby kind of wish and it was all to do with nice warm milk and lots of it!

The next special thing that happened was seeing, not one but two, glossy and sleek lucky black cats scamper across in front of them in the park.

"Quick, make a wish!" cried Katie.

So they all held hands again; Harry was a bit wriggly this time, but they managed to hold on to his hand.

Katie and Will wished again for a cute, fluffy, adorable kitten.

Jack wished for a birthday cake that was as big as the moon and looked like a red racing car.

Harry again had thoughts of warm milk, but also this time he wished for a cuddly toy giraffe and maybe a few things to chew on would be very nice too!

The third incident involved a little four-leaf clover that Jack found in the garden when they were playing 'sleeping lions'. He just lay down on the grass and there it was right under his nose.

"Look, you guys," Jack called. "Look what I've found," he continued as he thrust the little leaf towards Will and Katie.

Harry thought it looked like something that might be good to eat, but then Harry generally thought that everything and anything was good to eat!

The clover leaf was perfect, and when Will and Katie showed it to Aunty Leanne, she said:

"This will bring you all good luck!"

So they decided to make a wish again.

Katie and Will closed their eyes tightly and wished once more, as hard as they could, for a little, white, fluffy, cuddly, adorable kitten; Jack wished for a big chocolate snack bar, some jelly sweets that taste of bubble gum and a bag of chips; and Harry, well he had actually gone to sleep by now, so the other three children made a wish for him, which I think would make him smile, because what the others wished for was a musical mobile to go over Harry's cot and help him to get to sleep at night; I think Aunty Leanne and Uncle Simon would like that wish too!

The week flew by for Will and Katie as they were having such a great time with their cousins. It was now Friday and they would be going home in the morning. They had packed their bags and were getting ready for bed.

"It's been a brilliant week, hasn't it?" asked Will.

"Yes, really great!" agreed Katie.

"But I'll be very pleased to see Mum in the morning!" they both said in unison, and then burst out laughing.

They found it hard to sleep that night. They were both thinking about what a great week it had been, but also thinking about Mum and hoping she was OK. They had missed her and couldn't wait to tell her all about their week of fun with the boys.

It was getting quite dark when they both glanced out of the bedroom window and saw the most glorious shooting star.

"Wow!" said Katie.

"Wow, and double wow!" said Will.

"Quick, make a wish!" they both shouted together.

They wished as hard as they could.

"If there is anyone out there listening, please, please, please send us a fluffy, soft, gorgeous, little white kitten."

And with that, they both fell into a deep, deep, dreamless sleep.

Chapter Three

Will and Katie woke up bright and early the following morning. As a special treat for their last breakfast with their cousins, Aunty Leanne had made waffles with syrup and custard, their favourite combination.

"Yum!" they both said, followed by a quick:

"Thank you very much!"

Jack was enjoying this breakfast treat too, but Harry seemed to have most of his breakfast round his mouth, in his hair, all over his highchair and on the floor!

It's a good job that Aunty Leanne and Uncle Simon are laid back, the kids were both thinking as they looked at all the breakfast mess!

Harry just smiled contentedly amidst the chaos.

Mum came for them mid-morning, and she stopped for a chat and a cup of tea; Jack asked for 'coffee and cake'.

But Aunty Leanne laughed and said:

"I think milkshake and cake is best for you three."

Jack had been spending too much time with Doods, which is what the kids called their Granddad, because he wasn't like other Granddads,he was 'super cool'.

Doods always had to have coffee and cake at very regular intervals throughout the day!

Doods knew all about animals and flowers and trees, and well basically, Doods knew all there was to know about pretty much anything!

He was also a brilliant bird artist which was super, super cool!

Baby Harry soon woke up, and he was happy with his usual nice warm bottle of milk and a rusk.

"Well, it's time we made a move; you two, say bye-bye and thank you very much to Aunty Leanne, Uncle Simon and the boys for giving you a brilliant week," said Mum.

"Thank you so much, it's been a great week," said Will.

"Yes, it's been really good fun," added Katie.

"See you all soon," they called as they headed for the car.

Jack was jumping up and down and waving frantically in the doorway, as Harry bounced up and down in Aunty Leanne's arms, nearly launching himself headfirst into the flower bed!

The journey home was going to be pretty boring, the kids thought, as Will had forgotten to charge up his tablet and Katie had forgotten to bring her iPod. They decided to play 'I Spy', then started telling made-up stories to each other, then played 'first one to see', then Katie said, "Let's play hide and seek," at which Will and Mum burst into fits of laughter.

To settle the kids down for the rest of the journey, Mum put on a CD, and they all sang along at the top of their voices; so in the end, they actually had a good time and were soon back home.

The kids had got the whole weekend before going back to school. They couldn't wait to see their friends and tell them about all the weird and wonderful things that had happened while they were away!

Mum had got them some new bedding while they had been away seeing their cousins. Katie had turquoise and white with butterflies all over it. She was thrilled. Will had green and blue stripes which he thought was really 'cool!'

The kids decided to spend some time in their room and try and come up with another plan to persuade Mum to get the kitten they so desperately longed for. They were each lying on their own bed thinking of a master plan.

"Stop it, Will!" Katie called over to her brother.

"Stop what?" Will replied, feeling puzzled.

"You know what," said Katie in response.

Will didn't understand and looked over towards his sister; she was glaring at him.

"I haven't got a clue what you're going on about," he said, feeling pretty annoyed.

"These," said Katie, holding up a handful of white feathers. "You threw them at me."

"What???" said Will. "Are you mad? I didn't throw anything."

"Then how come I've got feathers on my bed?" said Katie.

"Search me!" said Will.

They were both very puzzled.

Why had Katie suddenly got feathers on her bed, and where had they come from? Very strange!!!

The kids couldn't come up with a good plan to try and make Mum get the kitten they both wanted so much, and so in the end they decided to go out and play. That night they both had strange dreams, but couldn't really explain them the next morning.

Chapter Four

It was Sunday and Mum asked them to sort out their uniforms for Monday morning. *Boring,* they both thought, but decided to get on with the job, and get it out of the way early so they could go out and play.

Suddenly, Mum was bellowing up the stairs.

"That was not funny!"

"What?" they both replied.

"Don't play innocent with me," said Mum. "You know what, feathers!"

The children looked at each other, they were both thinking the same thing. *Weird!*

"We don't know anything about feathers," Will replied.

"Well, how on Earth did these feathers suddenly appear in the lounge? White feathers all over the nice clean rug?"

"We don't know," the children replied together.

Most strange, they both thought.

What's going on? they both wondered.

That night, there were more feathers in the bedroom and in the upstairs hall. Then the following morning, they were in the bathroom sink!

Very strange! the kids thought again.

Mum was convinced that they were responsible however much they pleaded their innocence.

The kids headed off to school and didn't think much more about the feathers, as it was a very busy day.

When they got home, there were more feathers in their room, and later on in the evening they saw feathers in the downstairs hall and then in the dining room and more still in the kitchen; not many, just five or six small fluffy ones.

The feathers were all white, and just seemed to appear from nowhere.

They were feeling a bit spooked, and Mum was still convinced that they were behind these strange feather appearances.

What on Earth was going on?

They lay in bed that night trying to make sense of all this strangeness. Feathers were appearing from thin air that was very, very weird!

Again that night, they both had very vivid dreams but when they woke up, neither of them could explain what their dream had been about.

They headed off to school and decided not to tell any of their friends in case they thought Will and Katie were going 'bonkers'.

When they got home that night, they were very glad to find no more feathers in the house.

Maybe the weirdness was over, they thought.

They were looking forward to a nice relaxing evening playing on the Wii.

Needless to say, Mum had some thoughts of her own about this plan, and it went something like this:

"When they had done their homework, of course!

And put their uniforms away, of course!

And got their school bags ready for the next day, of course!"

The kids had eaten their dinner, and Mum was in the kitchen when she called through,

"Who's been messing with my perfume spray?"

"What?" The kids both called back.

"I can smell perfume!" called Mum.

"Don't know what you mean," said Will, "we haven't touched anything."

"Don't give me that," said Mum in reply, "I can smell something flowery and sweet."

The kids both looked at each other, raised their eyebrows, shrugged their shoulders and thought, *Mums!*

They were enjoying a game of bowling on the Wii when they both started sniffing.

"What's that smell?" said Katie.

"Don't know," replied Will.

"It smells like flowers," he added.

"But there aren't any flowers in here," Katie replied, feeling spooked again.

First, it was feathers, now the smell of flowers wafting through the house. The kids both thought something weird was going on but they had no idea what!

The rest of the evening was uneventful, thankfully. The kids really enjoyed their game and when Mum suggested it was bedtime, they tumbled into bed without complaint; which was most unusual!

The following day, Mum said,

"It's a beautiful crisp morning, let's walk to school instead of going in the car."

"OK," Will and Katie both replied whilst looking at each other with horrified expressions, and both thinking, *Oh no, that sounds like far too much exercise, and before the day has even really begun!*

They didn't make a fuss though because they were still trying to win Mum round to their way of thinking, that a kitten, particularly a small, fluffy, white one was just what they all needed to make life perfect.

Anyway, they packed their school bags with all they needed: lunch, PE kit, and all the various bits and bobs that were vital to get them through the day at school; which in Katie's case meant a vast selection of coloured hair clips, a variety of hair scrunchies and two flavoured lip balms!

As Katie picked up her coat off the armchair, a single beautiful white feather floated up to the ceiling and then came down to rest in her upturned hand.

Here we go again, she thought.

"Hurry up, you two," Mum called.

So Katie ran out to the car, putting thoughts of feathers out of her mind.

Will was hunting for his football kit. He was sure he had put it tidily away, clean and folded in his chest of drawers, but no, here it was all muddy and scrunched up under his bed; he wondered who could have put it there because he knew it couldn't possibly have been him! I think Mum would have a very different viewpoint entirely, but anyway, as he pulled the crusty mess from under his bed, a single, beautiful white feather flew up and then drifted back down towards him, *Uh-oh!* he thought. *Here we go again!*

Just then, Mum bellowed up the stairs, "We're going to be late, get a move on." So Will put thoughts of feathers out of his mind too.

They set off for school. It was a chilly morning, but as Mum had rightly said earlier, it was a gorgeous day for January. The kids were playing 'don't walk on the cracks' when they heard Mum exclaim, "Oh, how beautiful, but I would have thought it was far too early!" The kids both looked up to see what Mum was talking about, and there, fluttering beside them was the most exquisite, vividly coloured butterfly they had ever seen. It was a bit like a Red Admiral and a Peacock all rolled into one, but much bigger. "Must have escaped from the Butterfly Farm in town," Mum decided. The kids were enthralled by this superb sighting, but the butterfly seemed to suddenly vanish into thin air, it was most puzzling!

Katie turned to Will and said, "Did you see feathers again this morning?"

"Yes, I saw one really beautiful white feather when I was looking for my football kit."

"I saw one too," said Katie, "when I was getting my coat." They both thought hard about what this was all about; feathers appearing from nowhere, nice flowery smells for no apparent reason and now an amazing vanishing butterfly!

The day at school was like any other: singing (good), maths (dreadful), literacy time (OK), R.E. (awful), then P.E. (great fun).

Mum had brought the car to take them home as the day had turned quite dull, and there was a chilly breeze. Will and Katie were just about to sling their school bags into the boot when they spied another amazing butterfly. It had appeared as if by magic. "Maybe it had been trapped in the boot!" Will exclaimed. The butterfly was another beauty, with pearly white wings and a long floaty kind of tail that looked almost as if it were made of feathers. The kids were just about to call Mum to come and have a look when the butterfly seemed to vanish, just like the one they had seen earlier. Will and Katie looked at each other.

"Things are getting weirder and weirder round here," muttered Will.

"I'm feeling really spooked," Katie added.

They jumped into the car and headed home for dinner. As always, they were 'starving!' Dinner was great, Katie's favourite; pasta with pesto sauce and garlic bread. *Yum! she thought.*

Will and Katie decided to go up to their room and chill out before bath time. They jostled each other on the stairs playfully and burst into their room, laughing.

"What the...?" said Will in surprise.

"Oh my goodness!" blurted Katie.

There on the windowsill in their room was another stunning butterfly; it was huge, almost the size of a small bird; it had pearlescent wings in a deep shade of purple, and a kind of marbled pattern on its body in shades of mauve, pink and cream. The kids had never seen anything so beautiful. They were speechless and stared at the butterfly in stunned silence! When they had recovered a little, they both crept forward, trying to get closer to this lovely creature; Katie reached out to gently touch, but just as her fingers were about

to brush against the butterfly, it rose up into the air and swooped towards the ceiling in one graceful movement, and then completely vanished! "Oh no!" the kids cried together.

"Where's it gone?" puzzled Katie.

"It must be here somewhere," replied Will.

They looked everywhere, but the magnificent butterfly was nowhere to be seen. "Mum thinks these butterflies have escaped from the Butterfly Farm," stated Will. "I'm not so sure," he added.

"We've been to visit the Butterfly Farm, but never seen anything as amazing as the butterflies we keep seeing," said Katie. "And anyway, they seem to be able to vanish, and how did this one manage to get into our room?" She added, "The window was shut!"

"Very, very puzzling," they both agreed.

The kids decided to go downstairs and ask Mum if they could watch a DVD before bedtime. Thoughts of feathers, perfume, and butterflies were swimming around in their minds, but they just couldn't make any sense of what was going on, so they both decided to just relax and watch the film. Soon it was time for bath and bed. The kids both had vivid dreams again that night, all about giant butterflies and feathers raining down on them, but when they woke up, they couldn't quite remember any of the details. Anyway, there were school bags to sort out and swimming kit to pack and P.E. kit to find, which was probably under the bed again!

And more hair clips, scrunchies and lip balms!

Will and Katie had breakfast; yummy chocolate brioche that Nanny had given to them. They then got ready for school. There was so much to think about in class that thoughts of butterflies were not at the front of their minds. After lunch, Will had got P.E; he hated this lesson, almost as much as he hated maths and R.E.; all that mindless running around and climbing up ropes. He'd much rather be playing on his keyboard and writing new songs, but, *Oh well*, he thought to himself, *soon be home time*. Just as he was walking along a bench for the umpteenth time, he noticed something high up near the ceiling of the hall, something glittering and moving about. No one else seemed to notice, which Will thought was strange! He looked again and realised it was another one of the massive colourful butterflies; this one was of a glorious golden colour, with cream and pale green markings on the enormous wings. Will was about to shout out to his classmates, "Look, can't you see, look, look up there, what's the matter with you all?" But it really was quite obvious that he was the only one who could see this amazing creature! He couldn't wait to tell Katie at the end of the afternoon.

Will was very puzzled about why it was that he, Katie and Mum could see the butterflies when, apparently. No one else had any idea they existed!

Meanwhile, Katie had got swimming. She loved this part of the week. It was her favourite lesson; *Certainly miles better than 'stinky' phonics or boring writing practice,* she thought to herself. She was really glad that she had remembered her new pink goggles and sporty swimsuit; she thought she looked pretty awesome! Katie started to open her locker to put her clothes away, but as soon as she opened the door, *Wow, what was that?* she thought. Something large and fluttery and bright silver flew straight at her, she ducked and then turned to look up. Of course, it was another giant butterfly. *Oh my goodness, just wait 'til Will hears about this, he won't believe it!* Katie thought to herself. Of course she had no idea that Will was having a similar experience himself in his P.E. lesson.

The butterfly vanished as quickly as it had appeared, and Katie went into the pool for her lesson. She had a great session, winning most of the races, and thoughts of butterflies soon left her mind.

That evening, the kids told each other about the butterflies they had seen in school; they both wondered what they might mean! They both agreed that life was becoming full of strange and mysterious happenings. Little did they know that the biggest, most amazing and mysterious incident of all was about to take place, and that life would never be quite the same again.

Chapter Five

Will and Katie both felt particularly tired that evening. Mum said it was probably because of the P.E. and swimming sessions they had taken part in that afternoon. Somehow the kids weren't convinced, but they both had an overwhelming need to have an early night, which was MOST unusual!

They settled down comfortably under their snuggly duvets; Katie cuddled her big, fluffy dog and Will curled up with 'Brown Bear', which his great granddad, Tom, had given him when he was a baby. Sleep came quite quickly, and they both had a deep and refreshing dreamless night's sleep. Katie stirred first the following morning; before she opened her eyes, she thought, *What's that lovely smell? It's as if I've been sleeping in a flower garden!*

Will began to wake up just at that moment. He, too, thought, *Oh, what a wonderful smell, it's as if I've woken up in the local florists.* The children both lay still, enjoying the lovely and unexpected start to their day. Both of them felt a wonderful sense of calm and relaxation as they inhaled the wonderful floral aroma.

Within minutes, they both became aware of a strange sound in their room. It was a bit like a purring sound, but not quite. It was a bit like a rumbling sound, but not quite.

It was very quiet and soothing.

Sort of like having your hair very gently and repeatedly brushed, thought Katie. *Sort of like feeling a soft, warm breeze gently blowing against your skin,* thought Will.

They both decided in their own minds, quite quickly, that it was really like nothing they had ever experienced before. It was as if they could actually feel the sound humming inside them.

It was a lovely, warm, comforting feeling that they didn't ever want to end, and they hadn't even opened their eyes yet!

Will sleepily began to open his eyes. Katie was just starting to open hers too when they both became aware of a movement on the rug between their bed. They both blinked, as if to chase away their sleepiness, before taking another look.

"Oh my word!" exclaimed Will, in shock.

"What on earth?" added Katie, feeling completely bewildered.

On the rug, just a few inches away from them was a...well, they didn't know quite what it was! It was small, very small; no bigger than a new born puppy, but it clearly wasn't a puppy. It had a coat of, what appeared to be, a cross between fur and downy feathers. It was the most beautiful pearly white colour, just like the inside of an exotic seashell. The wonderful scent and soft relaxing rumble seemed to be coming from this fantastic, puzzling creature. Just as the kids were trying to make sense of what they were seeing, the situation became even more amazing! The beautiful tiny creature turned and gazed at them with the most enormous round blue eyes that they had ever seen.

By this time, Will and Katie were wide awake, sitting up in bed in stunned silence. They were both trying to take in what they were seeing. Just when they were sure nothing more curious or out of this world could happen, the little creature stretched its tiny legs, arched its perfect little back, and started to rise up into the air for an inch or two, before slowly settling back down onto the rug. The kids could not believe their eyes; it just couldn't be possible, they must still be fast asleep and this was all a wonderful dream, they both decided. What they had seen was a pair of the most perfect, tiny, beautiful wings attached to the back of this perfect, tiny, beautiful creature! Will and Katie were both speechless, sitting, staring open-mouthed at the magic of it all.

They were both quite sure now that absolutely nothing else out of this world could happen, when they heard the most lovely musical little voice chiming inside their minds saying the words: "Hello, Will and Katie, my name is Pearly, and I'm your Kitty Angel."

The kids' thoughts were in a whirl!

Question after question whizzed in and out of their minds:

What could this creature be?

Where is it from?

How did it get here?

Why has it come?

When did it arrive?

They were completely buzzing with the shock and excitement of what was happening to them!

Will was the first to gather his thoughts and actually ask Pearly a question.

"Where have you come from, Pearly?" Will queried, looking deep into Pearly's enormous, mesmerising blue eyes.

Again, Pearly's beautiful, bell-like voice came into Will and Katie's minds, saying, "I have come from the world of Angels."

Angels! the kids both thought.

"But surely that's all made up?" said Will.

"Like fairy stories," added Katie.

"And space creatures!" blurted Will.

Pearly laughed, and the sound in their heads was like soft warm rain falling gently.

"There are many beings in existence," replied Pearly. "Not all can be seen, or felt, or heard by everyone; you must make up your own minds," she added.

"Where do you live?" Will asked.

"I live on the pink clouds, the ones you can sometimes see at dawn and dusk, the ones that look like pink candy floss up in the sky," Pearly replied.

"But how can you live on a cloud???" Katie spluttered.

"Because I'm a Kitty Angel," replied Pearly. "I'm not like you and Will," she added, "I have special Angelic powers."

The kids found what they were hearing all very hard to take on board.

"Well, we can both see you," cried Katie.

"And we can both hear you!" exclaimed Will.

So we know you are not in our imagination, they both thought.

"How did you get into our room?" asked Katie. "The doors and windows are all locked, and we didn't hear you arrive, you were just sort of here when we woke up."

"You called for me," Pearly replied, "and that made it possible for me to come into your world, and into your home." Pearly continued, "Your pleas caused our worlds to open up to each other for the smallest of moments, and as I am a very small creature, I was able to pass through; that's how it works."

"I don't need open windows or doors, as I have explained already, I have Angelic powers."

Wow, thought Katie.

Cool, thought Will.

"But we didn't call for you," said Will, feeling perplexed.

"Oh, but you did," replied Pearly, "let me explain. Do you remember the rainbow you saw at half-term?" Pearly asked.

"Yes," the kids both replied at once.

"Do you remember the lucky black cats you also saw at half-term?"

"Yes," the kids both replied in harmony.

"Do you remember the four-leaf clover that your cousin Jack found at half-term?"

"Yes, we do," Will and Katie exclaimed.

"And finally, do you remember the glorious shooting star that you both saw at half-term?"

"Yes, yes, yes," the kids both squealed.

The kids both thought back fondly to the half-term holiday they had with their cousins Jack and Harry; it was a magical time.

"Well, there you are!" said Pearly, "that's what it takes to call a Kitty Angel down from the pink clouds; four magical signs and the heartfelt wishes from a child or children in need."

Katie and Will didn't want to be rude and they didn't know quite what to say, because what they had clearly and desperately wished for had been a little, white, gorgeous and cuddly white kitten, not a Kitty Angel!!!

Just then, they heard Mum coming up the stairs. They both glanced at each other, and then at Pearly.

"Oh no, it's time to get ready for school, and Mum will be bursting through that door at any moment," cried Will.

"Pearly, quick, hide!" spluttered Katie.

At which point, Mum came flying into their bedroom.

The kids leapt up and tried to conceal their unexpected, and very unusual little visitor, but it was too late, *Mum must be able to see her clearly,* they both thought.

What will she say? thought Katie unhappily.

What will she do? thought Will, feeling sure it wouldn't be anything with a happy ending.

"Come on, you two, time you were up and getting dressed, breakfast is ready. I'll see you downstairs in two ticks, OK!" said Mum.

What the dickens...? thought Will.

What! Has Mum gone blind? thought Katie.

Mum hadn't even mentioned the beautiful, magical and extremely unusual creature sitting there in full view on the rug!!!

The kids were both relieved, but very puzzled, and turned to Pearly hoping for some kind of explanation.

"Well, it's like this," Pearly began to explain. "Most adults just aren't able to see me, it's as simple as that! Only if an adult really believes in Angels, and regularly receives their own Angel signs, will they sometimes be able to see me."

Brilliant! the kids both thought. *That makes life a lot easier.*

Will and Katie both knew that Mum didn't believe in Angels, and now they understood that this was the reason why she hadn't been able to see Pearly.

Will and Katie were feeling so relieved Mum couldn't see their Kitty Angel that it didn't even occur to them to think about any of the other adults in the family. Katie suddenly had a thought, "Were the feathers and butterflies all to do with you?" she asked. "Oh, and the smell of perfume that was all around the house at times?" she added.

"Yes," replied Pearly. "Let me explain: when a gap is starting to appear between my world and yours, elements of my world can slip into your world. That's why you found white feathers; as you can imagine, we have a lot of white feathers in my world!

"The scent too, that was coming from my world. We have flowers everywhere; they're not like most of the flowers here in your world, our flowers all have a very special quality that brings tranquillity and peace."

"What about the amazing butterflies, were they from your world too?" asked Will. "Mum said they were from the Butterfly Farm, but I have never seen anything so amazing and beautiful in there before," he added.

"Ah, yes, the butterflies," said Pearly thoughtfully, "now how can I explain about the butterflies?" she pondered. "I think the best way to describe the butterflies is as scouts. When a Kitty Angel is coming to your world," Pearly continued, "we need to be sure it will be safe for us; we need to be sure that we are really needed and so our butterflies come ahead of us to have a look, and then they come back and report to us."

"Right, I see," said Will.

Katie suddenly had a thought, 'But Mum saw the feathers, she saw the butterflies and she could smell the perfume!'

"That's right," said Pearly, "because you are all part of the same family, your Mum, and any of your relatives for that matter, would be able to see the feathers and butterflies, and smell the flowers, but usually only the children in a family can see me."

"Right, I understand," said Katie.

"So that means Jack and Harry will be able to see you when we next get together, brilliant!" exclaimed Will.

The kids had a mad rush to get ready for school before Mum came back upstairs and gave them a good telling off.

They could hardly eat their breakfast they were so excited; they could hardly get their school bags sorted they were so excited; and they nearly forgot their packed lunches they were so excited!

Their minds were buzzing with thoughts of Kitty Angel: the magic of her, the wonder of her and the fun they were going to have with their new and very magical pet! Though they were both very sure that she was much, much more than just a pet!

Chapter Six

The school day was a complete blur for both the kids. How were they supposed to concentrate on maths and writing and RE and all the other boring school subjects? All they could think about was Pearly, their very own Kitty Angel.

Pearly didn't go to school. She said she would be far too much of a distraction for them both.

Thankfully, home time came round quite quickly; the kids were ecstatic at the thought of seeing Pearly again and finding out more about her.

When Mum turned up at school to collect Will and Katie, she was in quite a good mood. The kids had got used to Mum being a bit moody these days and so they were very pleased to see her smiling.

They quickly threw their belongings into the boot of the car and settled into the back seat together, without even arguing about who was going to sit in the front! Mum was very surprised, and very pleased too, that there wasn't the usual bickering about whose turn it was to go in the front. The kids both felt too excited to argue, and they wanted to sit together so they could whisper about Pearly without Mum hearing them.

Mum put the radio on and started to hum along. *Gosh,* the kids both thought, *what's got into Mum?* They decided not to say anything for fear of spoiling the mood and ruining the evening, which had got off to such a good start for all of them.

Soon, they were home, and the minute they were out of the car, they went flying up the path to get into the house.

"Hey, you two!" Mum called after them. "What about your bags?" In their haste to get into the house, they had completely forgotten to get their belongings out of the boot of the car. We're in for it now, they both thought in dismay.

"Never mind, I'll bring them in, you two carry on," said Mum.

What? No telling off, no punishment, no scowling look? thought Will.

This is great. Whatever is going on with Mum, I really like it, thought Katie.

They dashed upstairs to the bedroom and there was their beautiful, adorable, tiny little Kitty Angel, Pearly. They just stood and stared at her in awe and wonder. They had half expected her to be gone, half expected her to be nothing but a wonderful dream, half expected to be very, very disappointed. But no, there she was curled up on Katie's bed, making her lovely rumbling kind of purring sound, which they could both feel right inside them.

Pearly opened her amazing, enormous, round blue eyes, gave a little stretch, had a little flutter off the bed and then settled back down.

"Hello, you two, how was school?" said Pearly.

"School was school," said Will. "Boring as ever," he added.

"It was OK," said Katie, "but all I've been thinking about all day was getting home to see you, Pearly," she continued.

"What shall we do now then?" asked Will. "Are you going to do some marvellous, magical things, Pearly?" he queried.

"Haven't you two got homework?" Pearly enquired.

"Homework!" spluttered Will.

"Yes, but..." Katie started to protest.

Pearly quickly responded, "Life goes on, and some things just have to be done. One of those things, I'm afraid, is homework!"

The kids were very disappointed, as they were expecting all sorts of fun and games with their new little friend.

"I suppose we'd better get on then," said Katie. "The sooner we start, the quicker we'll be finished," she added.

Will agreed, and so they went down stairs to get their school bags.

"Do you two want a drink and a snack?" Mum asked, as the kids went into the lounge to get their homework.

"Yes, please, Mum," they both chorused.

The atmosphere in the house was subtly different. *There was a kind of peacefulness now,* the kids both thought.

Mum came through with squash and biscuits and asked if they needed any help, as she had a bit of spare time before starting dinner.

"Thanks, Mum, but I think we'll be fine," Katie said, thinking, *How lovely. Mum hasn't offered any help with homework for as long as I can remember!*

The kids both wanted to get back upstairs to be with their little Kitty Angel.

At least having Pearly with them would help to make the homework a bit less boring, they both thought.

They had their snack and drink and then settled down to work on their school projects.

Katie was working on Victorian Britain; she had to research the lives of Victorian children and write a little piece about either a rich child or a poor child, and then do a drawing. *This is interesting, but it's going to take ages,* she thought to herself. "Oh well, better make a start," she said to Will.

Will was working on a project about France; his teacher had visited the country quite often and was very keen to teach her class about life in France.

Will had got to research the differences between French and British food; then he had got to make up a typical French menu, and compare it to a typical British menu. *Not too bad, I suppose,* he thought to himself. "This will probably take me most of the evening," Will said to Katie.

They were both thinking that they would have very little time to play with Pearly, but 'hey-ho, that's life'.

"I'm going to start dinner now," Mum called up to them. "It'll be done in about forty minutes, OK?" she added.

"Yes, Mum," they shouted in reply.

They were both thinking that this wouldn't give them much time to get stuck into their homework!

Pearly just seemed to be curled up asleep on Will's bed, the lovely rumbling sound she made was quietly buzzing away inside both their heads; it was very soothing. They both started researching their homework projects; Will on his Samsung Tablet and Katie on her iPod Touch.

It was all very strange, very weird and very puzzling, because they just began to work on their individual projects, expecting to be slogging away for ages when they realised that they had actually finished all the work that needed to be done! Pearly stretched and yawned and did a lovely little fluttering movement up towards the ceiling, gently moving her divine tiny wings. "All done then?" she asked, as she settled down on to the rug.

The kids were bemused. "Did you do something, Pearly?" Katie asked.

"Our homework seemed to sort of do itself," Will added.

"Well, we don't want to be stuck up here all evening working, do we?" Pearly said with a little chuckle.

"Brilliant," said Will.

"Fantastic," added Katie.

They now had the whole evening to play and chill out. They couldn't quite believe their luck, but what they did know was that life seemed to be getting better and better since their very own Kitty Angel had come into their lives!

"Dinner's ready, you two," Mum called up to them.

Perfect, they both thought.

After dinner, they had a great time reading, playing games with Pearly and generally relaxing, and soon it was time for a lovely bath and bed.

Chapter Seven

The rest of the week whizzed by in much the same way: Mum in a good mood; homework done in a flash; Pearly divine, and very playful; lovely dinners, and at the end of each day, deep dreamless sleep.

There was a calm and happy kind of atmosphere in the house now, which the kids felt sure must be something to do with Pearly, their adorable little Kitty Angel. The weekend was coming up and they were really excited about going to see their cousins, Jack and Harry. They always had a smashing time on these visits; Aunty Leanne made them a fab Victoria sponge to share, and Uncle Simon got them some great films to watch and new games to play on his iPad. Jack was brilliant fun to play with, and Harry was starting to join in a bit more now rather than sleeping most of the time; his contribution consisted mainly of flapping his arms and shouting out different sounds, and when he wasn't in his seat, he would be rolling around on the floor and giggling.

Saturday morning arrived and they gobbled their breakfast down so that they could get ready quickly to go on their visit. They looked around for Pearly, but couldn't see her anywhere. *Odd,* they both thought. Mum was calling to them to "come and get in the car", so they had to dash downstairs, feeling a bit disappointed that they couldn't take Pearly with them.

It didn't take long to get to their cousins' house and soon, they were knocking on their front door.

They could hear Jack shouting excitedly in the background, "Billy, Katie, Billy, Katie!" as Aunty Leanne opened the front door.

The minute they were through the door, Jack ran full pelt down the hall and gave the kids both a great big hug; they really did all love each other very much!

Then Uncle Simon appeared carrying Harry, whose arms were flapping and legs were kicking, and surprise, surprise, there hovering just above Harry was their own beautiful, tiny little Kitty Angel, Pearly!

They were delighted. *This would make the day even more perfect, having Pearly with them,* they both thought.

Will and Katie both suddenly had the same dreadful thought, 'How would they be able to stop Jack from saying something about Pearly to Mum, Uncle Simon and Aunty Leanne?'

Jack was looking up at Pearly in absolute wonder.

The adults were too busy chatting to notice Jack pointing and gasping in delight at the wonderful creature he had just spotted.

Will and Katie were desperately trying to think of what to do to prevent Jack from saying anything when they heard a little sound inside both of their heads that was a bit like bells jingling, and a bit like a shaken tambourine.

Suddenly, Jack said, "Come on, you two, see my new green tractor."

Not a word about Pearly, who was still fluttering around a very delighted Harry. *Most puzzling!* they both thought, feeling very relieved nevertheless.

The kids all went into the front room while the adults headed for the kitchen and cups of tea. Uncle Simon brought Harry through and put him into his special chair; Pearly was still fluttering around him and so Will and Katie were amazed that Jack didn't say anything!

"What would you three like to drink?" said Uncle Simon.

"Coke!" shouted Jack.

"I don't think so, young man," Uncle Simon replied, laughing.

"We've got squash, apple juice, milkshake..."

Before he could say another word, the kids all shouted in unison:

"Milkshake, please!"

Uncle Simon went back to the kitchen to get their drinks, and so now all the children were on their own with Pearly.

"Did you stop Jack from saying anything to the adults?" Will asked.

"Yes," Pearly replied. "It makes life easier for everyone. Adults don't usually believe little kids anyway when they talk about kittens with wings, they just think it's all in their imagination, and say, 'How sweet.' So I thought it best to be on the safe side."

"Great," said Will.

Jack now dashed over to Harry and was trying to catch a very fluttery Kitty Angel; he was calling, "Kitty, kitty flying!" with a look of wonder and delight on his face.

"That's Pearly," Katie explained.

"She's a Kitty Angel," Will added.

"Kitty Angel, Kitty Angel!" Jack cried excitedly. "Flying, flying little kitty," he added.

As a three-year-old learning all about the world around him, he just accepted that this wasn't unusual at all, just normal and fine.

Just then, Aunty Leanne appeared with the drinks, and a piece of cake for all of them; well not for Harry as he was still just on baby milk, and anyway he had no teeth for cake. Harry was quite happy chewing on his toy and trying to grab the beautiful, fluttering creature that was just beyond his reach.

The adults spent most of the time in the kitchen drinking endless cups of tea and eating cake.

Mum seemed to be discussing something important with the other adults, because every time one of the kids wondered into the room, she stopped speaking and looked a bit odd!

Anyway, the day was great; Jack and Harry loved Pearly and they all had a fantastic time together.

Chapter Eight

The journey home seemed to whizz by; the kids had a bit of time to chill out and soon it was time for dinner.

"I'm going to be popping out for a little while this evening," Mum explained, as she was clearing up after dinner. "I won't be out for long, and Nanny is coming over to babysit."

Nanny, fantastic! the kids both thought.

They loved their Nanny; she was great fun to be with never told them off and always brought them treats.

"If you both have your bath a bit earlier than normal and get ready for bed, then you can stay up a little bit later and have a chat with Nanny," Mum said.

It was six o'clock when the doorbell chimed, "Nanny's here," the kids both shouted up to Mum, whilst at the same time dashing to open the door.

"Hello, Nanny!" they bellowed, as they were both trying to hug their Nanny at the same time. "Hello, you two!" their Nanny replied with a big smile on her face. "And how are you two horrors?" she added, laughing.

"We're fine, Nanny," said Will.

"We're really pleased to see you, Nanny," said Katie. "Will Doods be coming over later?" she added.

"Oh, it's lovely to see you two and your mum; it seems like ages since we had a get together. I'm afraid Doods isn't home from his trip yet, but I spoke to him earlier today and he sends you all his love. I'm sure he'll be popping in to see you when he gets back and tell you all about the Outer Hebrides."

Doods loved wild places and bird watching, and often went away on trips for a few days to take photographs of birds. He then spent time painting fantastic watercolours. This latest trip was lasting a bit longer though and the kids were both really missing him!

Just then, Mum came down the stairs and she looked amazing.

"Wow! Mum, you look fab!" shouted Katie.

"You look very glam, Mum," said Will.

"Thanks, kids," said Mum.

"You look positively glowing," added their Nan, and the kids thought they saw her wink, but surely not!

Mum set off on her night out, and the kids did wonder for a while where she might be going; they guessed it was out with one of her friends from work, although she didn't usually look quite so glam when it was a 'girls' night out.

They soon put thoughts of Mum out of their minds though as they were having fun with Nan.

First, they did a little show; which mainly consisted of Katie practicing her gymnastics, and nearly doing herself a serious injury hitting the sofa!

I'd better not get hurt, Katie thought to herself. Katie really loved her gymnastics sessions, and there was a gymnastics competition coming up in a couple of weeks; she was desperate to be in the squad and take part.

Will did manage to sing Nanny his new musical composition; he'd been working on this song for a while, trying to pick out a melody for it on his new keyboard. Will was involved with a concert at school, and although he was very excited, he was also terrified that something would go wrong on the day.

Mum kept saying, "Don't be daft, you're brilliant at music, and you've got a really great voice. Be confident, and all will go well I'm sure!"

Will was really hoping that Doods would be back from his trip to the Outer Hebrides in time for the concert; he tried very hard to stop worrying, and managed to push thoughts of the concert to the back of his mind for the moment.

A lot of the time that the kids were downstairs with Nanny, they were thinking of Pearly, who, as usual, was up in their bedroom. They both wished that Nanny would be able to see their Kitty Angel; they were sure that Nanny would understand and they longed to share their special and very magical secret with at least one adult.

They kept thinking about what Pearly had said, that most of the time only children could see her and that only occasionally would an adult be able to see a Kitty Angel!

The kids always told Nanny that she was just a 'big kid', but they guessed that acting like a kid didn't actually make you a kid!

But they both hoped it would be enough to enable Nanny to see their gorgeous little Kitty Angel, Pearly!

It was soon time for bed, well actually, long past their usual bedtime because they were having a great time playing on the Wii with Nan and then playing games on the Tablet and iPod and then playing hide and seek and then looking at cars in Will's magazine and ponies in Katie's magazine; it was all such fun!

Anyway, it was definitely time to be getting into bed, and so the kids headed up the stairs.

"Clean your teeth, and don't forget to brush for two minutes," Nanny called up to them. "I'll be up in a couple of minutes to read you a story and tuck you both in," she added.

The kids cleaned their teeth and washed their hands and then headed into the bedroom, knowing that Pearly would be in there waiting for them.

Pearly had said earlier that she would stay upstairs, as she wanted the kids to have special time with their Nanny without her fluttering about the room and distracting them.

Obviously, Pearly didn't know anything about Will and Katie's Nanny, she certainly didn't know how 'young at heart' their Nanny was, she didn't know that Nan was really open minded and believed in all sorts of things that a lot of adults just dismissed as 'hogwash'.

Throughout the evening though, Pearly had started to have a feeling about Nanny, a very good feeling. She had a strong sense that Will and Katie were about to find out just how unusual their Nanny really was!

Nanny started to come up the stairs; the kids were in their room and about to get into bed; Pearly was in her usual spot on the rug between the kids' beds; the kids were very relaxed. Pearly was curled up and rumbling quietly away inside their heads; all was calm, all was peaceful. Nanny came into their room to tuck them up, and then: shock! Horror! How can this be! Nan was looking at Pearly, Pearly was looking at Nan, and then:

"Hello, Nanny," said Pearly, "I'm Will and Katie's Kitty Angel, and my name is Pearly," she added.

The kids were both stunned. *What on Earth!* they both thought.

What's Pearly up to? thought Will.

How can Nanny see Pearly? thought Katie.

"Well," said Nanny, looking in wonder at the gorgeous, tiny little Kitty Angel. "Aren't you an absolute beauty!"

Will and Katie were speechless; Nanny wasn't running from the room, screaming in panic and tearing her hair out; Nanny was just looking at Pearly as if this was an everyday occurrence.

"A Kitty Angel, how absolutely divine!" Nanny continued.

"Nanny!" The kids both chimed together.

"You aren't supposed to be able to see Pearly!" they added.

"How the...?" spluttered Will.

Pearly was just sitting peacefully on the rug as Nanny bent down and started to stroke her tiny downy back. The rumbling sound coming from Pearly was loud and clear in all their heads, so calming and lovely!

"You two know that I have always believed in Angels," said Nanny, "you also know that I find white feathers on a regular basis, don't you?" she added.

"Yes, of course," the kids both said in reply.

"I'm not surprised at all that there are creatures such as this beautiful Kitty Angel."

"That's why Nanny can see me," Pearly added.

"Do you two remember what I said to you a while ago, that occasionally an adult can see a Kitty Angel?" Pearly asked.

"Oh, of course, I'd forgotten," Will replied.

"Oh yes, I remember now," Katie added.

"As she said, Nanny is always seeing white feathers, they just seem to be around wherever she goes," continued Will.

"Nanny has always told us that they're a sign that Angels are watching over us," said Katie.

"Nanny, it's brilliant that you can see Pearly too," said Will, feeling absolutely thrilled and delighted at this unexpected turn of events.

Katie was really pleased too and felt very happy about being able to share their special secret with Nanny.

They all snuggled down together on Katie's bed and Nanny read them a story that she'd made up especially for them.

Pearly was rumbling inside all their heads and the atmosphere in the room was one of complete peace. When the story was done, Will crept into his own bed and the children were soon fast asleep.

The next morning, they woke up early and got their school things ready quickly so they could play with Pearly before they had to go to school.

The kids could both hear Mum humming away in the kitchen.

The family were all having breakfast together when the phone rang. It was

Uncle Simon ringing to say that something very strange had happened. Harry had said his first word; it wasn't 'dada' as you would expect, or even 'mama'. Both he and Aunty Leanne were extremely puzzled, because what Harry had actually said, as clear as day was 'Kitty'! The kids could hear Mum telling Nanny, Nanny was trying hard not to react to this news, but she glanced across at the kids and gave a little knowing smile.

Apparently, when Harry said 'Kitty', Jack had started dancing round the room saying, "Kitty, Kitty, lovely little flying Kitty." Aunty Leanne had laughed and told him to get ready for nursery, and thought Jack was just being his usual entertaining self!

The kids both found this conversation very amusing.

Mum was popping out again that night so Nanny was having another sleep over. The atmosphere in the house continued to be a happy one; Mum was humming to herself, and she hadn't told the kids off for days now. It was fantastic, they both thought.

Will and Katie went upstairs to say 'bye' to Pearly. She was curled up in her usual place on the rug; she seemed to spend almost all the time up in their bedroom and didn't seem bored or lonely; they both wondered how she occupied her mind, and decided they would ask her that evening.

School went quickly, and when Mum came to pick the kids up, she looked amazing. "Mum, have you been to the hairdressers?' Katie yelled.

"Yes," said Mum, "I thought it was time to smarten myself up a bit." The kids both thought that their mum looked fab with her new haircut, and it even looked like she'd had a manicure as well!

They both started wondering what this could mean.

When they got home, Nanny looked really pleased, and she and Mum spent a lot of time chatting in the kitchen. Every time one of the kids popped in, there was a deathly silence.

The kids were wondering what was going on, but as Mum was happy, and Nanny was happy, they didn't feel worried.

They decided to do their express homework with Pearly, which had become part of their evening routine, and then they were going to ask her about her days.

Homework was done and dusted. Mum had brought them up a lovely snack and drink, and they were chilling out before dinner, bath and bedtime.

"Pearly, we both feel really sorry for you stuck in our room all day. It must be very boring and lonely for you," said Will.

"Yes, Pearly, we wish you would come to school with us, at least you wouldn't be on your own and what fun and games we could have!' added Katie.

Pearly started to chuckle to herself, and it felt like the most lovely tickling feeling inside their heads.

"What's so funny?" the kids asked. They both looked at their lovely little Kitty Angel, waiting for a response.

"Well, it's like this," Pearly began. "I am here in one sense, but in another sense, I'm not!"

The kids looked at each other, feeling completely puzzled!

"Let me explain," said Pearly. "I am here in your room in the physical sense, but my mind goes wandering all over the place."

"I don't really understand!" said Katie.

"That sounds a bit weird!" added Will.

"You have to remember that I'm not like you two, I'm a Kitty Angel, and as I've told you before, we have Angelic powers; our minds can sort of step outside our physical body and travel. It means I can be keeping an eye on your family and seeing that all is going well, and also I can go and see my Kitty Angel friends!" Pearly explained.

"Wow," the kids both exclaimed.

"And we were thinking you were stuck in this room all the time, being bored and lonely," said Katie.

The kids were both really glad that their Kitty Angel could travel about in her own special way. They were both wondering what she meant about 'All going well' and were about to ask her when Mum called up that dinner was ready.

By the time they had finished eating, had their bath and another lovely story from Nanny, they had both completely forgotten what it was that they wanted to ask Pearly.

"I'm off out now," Mum said, as she came up to tuck them in.

Both the kids thought how lovely Mum looked. She'd got a new dress on, and there was something about the look in her eye, a sort of happy and hopeful look, that really made the kids feel happy too!

"Have a good time, Mum," the kids both said.

"Thanks, you two. Be good for Nanny, and I hope you both sleep well," said Mum.

The kids snuggled down with the sound of Pearly rumbling in their heads, and soon they were sleeping soundly.

Chapter Nine

The day of the school concert was only a week away, and so Will was spending a lot of his spare time practising and trying to ensure that his song was perfect in every way. He had got the melody just right and was pretty pleased with the words too, although he never felt completely happy with anything he wrote. The hardest part was trying to keep calm. Will knew he was a pretty good singer, and everyone seemed to like his compositions. If only he didn't get the jitters when it came to performing.

Nanny suggested sniffing lavender oil to keep calm, but that made him stink all flowery, and the kids at school would mock him.

Mum said, "Try deep breathing," but that just made him go dizzy!

Katie just said, "Get a grip, Will." Such a 'loving' sister!

Katie's lack of sisterly support was largely due to the fact that she was really worried herself about the trials for the gym tournament. There were so many things that could go wrong: she could get an injury, she could mess up on one of the pieces of apparatus; she could get her mat routine and timing wrong; she could fall off during the bar exercise, but worst of all by far was the fact that she may not be chosen to take part at all. She didn't even want to think about that possibility.

The kids would take turns at night, telling Pearly about their worries and fears. Their little Kitty Angel had a really calming effect on them both even though she never offered advice, and she never ever told them not to be silly, or to pull themselves together or get a grip! There was just something about her that was very reassuring and made things feel OK. She was very much a part of their lives now, it felt as if she had always been there, quietly rumbling away.

The day of the concert arrived and Will was feeling quite calm, he had practised so much he felt confident that all would go well. Mum was full of praise for him, and that meant a lot.

Katie said, "Good luck, and break a leg, or should that be break a finger, ha–ha!"

School went well and it was soon time to go home. When Mum picked the kids up, she was in a very quiet mood; not grumpy or upset, she just seemed deep in thought. Will was very pleased when she said she was really looking forward to the concert that evening.

Will felt so calm he even surprised himself, he had expected to feel jittery with butterflies in his stomach.

I bet this is because of Pearly, he thought to himself.

When they all got home, the kids rushed upstairs to see their little Kitty Angel, expecting her to be on the rug curled up in her usual spot, but there was no sign of her!

How odd, thought Katie.

"I wonder where she could be?" said Will.

He had a funny little feeling start to creep into the very middle of him; he wasn't too keen on that feeling and tried to distract himself by teasing Katie, which didn't go down well at all.

"Dinner's ready," Mum called up to them soon after they got home.

"We need to eat early tonight because of Will's concert," she explained.

At the mention of the concert, Will had that feeling again, as if he had something buzzing and squirming right inside his stomach; he didn't like it, he didn't like it at all.

There was still no sign of Pearly, no comforting rumbling sound, no calming look from those enormous blue eyes.

It would soon be time to head over to the school hall to get ready and the very thought now was making Will feel really sick.

Maybe I'm coming down with a bug, Will thought to himself, he really was feeling far from OK.

Will went upstairs to get changed. He was thinking that if he got into his favourite pair of bright green chinos, his check shirt and red hoodie, maybe he would feel better!

Mum had made sure all his favourite clothes were clean and ironed for him, she knew how important his image was, particularly on these special occasions. Usually when he had his best outfit on, he felt more confident, but this didn't work today.

And where was Pearly?

I really need her tonight, thought Will, and he had a horrible feeling that his song was going to be really dreadful. In his mind he saw himself being booed off the stage, and that dreadful squirmy, buzzy, wriggly feeling right in his middle just kept on getting bigger and stronger.

"Time to get in the car," Mum called up.

Will thought he was going to be sick! "Mum, I'm not well!" he called down.

"You're fine," Mum called back, "just a bit of stage fright, that's all."

The journey to school went by in a flash.

There was a lot of hustle and bustle in the school hall as everything was being put in place for the evening's entertainment.

Will scanned the hall, looking up and down and in all the corners but could see no sign of Kitty Angel.

Where oh where was she, Will thought to himself; as his stomach churned, his hands trembled and his knees started knocking together.

Just as he was deciding if he needed to dash to the toilet to be sick, or dash out of the hall door and hide, he heard the sound of the school orchestra strike up the opening number.

There was something about the familiarity of the tune that had a calming effect on Will, after all he'd heard it lots of times during rehearsals.

He decided to stick around after all.

He also remembered that Nanny swore by peppermint tea for calming her stomach, so he decided to see if they had any on the refreshment stall.

He was in luck, and so sipping a warm and soothing cup, he listened to the next act in the school concert, which was a cute girl in his class who was singing a song he remembered from the Pop Choir he went to each week. She was brill!

Will was beginning to get into a more calm frame of mind when he glimpsed his mum out of the corner of his eye. She was beckoning to him and mouthing, in that strange exaggerated way that adults sometimes do:

"Time to get backstage, Will, you're on soon!"

He took one final look around the hall and thought he may have seen a swift shadow of Kitty Angel, but couldn't be sure.

He took a not too deep breath, remembering the dizzy spells, and started to walk towards the backstage area.

His mate, Andy, was tuning up, ready to go on and perform his guitar solo.

Will knew that after Andy it would be his turn to go out on stage and sing.

He didn't feel too bad now, what with peppermint tea and breathing, which he thought was, after all, a very good idea if you wanted to stay alive, ha-ha!

He knew he had practised enough.

He knew he could sing well.

He knew his song was good, he'd worked on it for ages.

He felt good in his outfit.

Mum was in the audience, which was smashing!

Katie was in the audience, which was, well maybe not quite so smashing!

But, well, to be fair to her she hadn't really said anything nasty in the car, and she had let him hold her special fluffy unicorn for good luck, so not such a dreadful sister after all, maybe!

The fleeting, shadowy glimpse of what may have been Kitty Angel didn't really stay in his mind; it was more like a soft and drifty cloud floating through his thoughts, breaking up and then reforming but insubstantial and nebulous!

There was applause and cheering as Andy came off stage grinning from ear to ear. He'd been a great success, and now it was Will's turn to step out onto the vast school stage and face his audience, and also his fears!

One of the teachers gave Will a reassuring smile and indicated it was time for him to perform.

As his keyboard was taken onto the stage, he sensed rather than saw Kitty Angel, but again it was a drifty kind of feeling.

He was quite calm now, and suddenly confident as he stepped out onto the stage and looked up to see Mum smiling, and so full of pride she seemed to be head and shoulders above everyone else, and there was Katie giving a thumbs up and holding her lucky unicorn where he could see it.

As Will started to play the opening chords of his song, he was completely lost in the music, and suddenly, as the time just flew by, he was coming to the final chorus.

There had been no missed chords.

There had been no forgotten words.

There had been no croaky voice.

It had been a near perfect performance, and as he sang his heart out in the last line, the audience erupted in applause, whistles, shouting, and cheering.

Mum and Katie were up on their feet clapping for all they were worth, and Will thought he could see a tear glistening on Mum's cheek!

He was elated!

He was thrilled!

He was over the moon!

He was also suddenly, completely exhausted and now just wanted to get home and unwind, and sleep.

What a night!

And was Kitty Angel part of it or not???

Most puzzling!

That night, Will had a deep sense of happiness and satisfaction and slept really well.

That is once Mum and Katie had finished heaping praise on him, it was, well, embarrassing!

Chapter Ten

The weekend soon came around and when they got up on Saturday morning, Pearly was nowhere to be seen. Will and Katie started to feel concerned that they hadn't seen her properly for a while when Mum surprised them both by saying, "Let's go and visit Grandma today."

Will and Katie adored their Grandma. She was Doods' Mum, and because she was getting frail, had recently moved to live near them in a special place where she could be independent, but get help if necessary; it was a perfect arrangement!

The kids quickly finished their breakfast and got ready to go. Mum said they would pick up some flowers and sweets on the way; Grandma loved flowers, the brighter the better! She also loved sweets, big boiled sweets that always sat temptingly in a little dish on her coffee table!

Grandma's flat was in a lovely big house, with a really pretty garden, where she could sit out in nice weather and where the kids could play hide and seek while she kept a loving eye on them.

The house had lots of elderly people living there, and they always loved to see Will and Katie.

It was a short journey via the florists and sweet shop, and so the kids were soon bounding through the front door of Grandma's building.

The first bit of fun was going up in the lift; Grandma lived on the top floor, so they got to have a good ride up which was great!

The next bit of fun was racing down the hall to Grandma's flat, which was at the very end of the hallway.

"Beat you, slow coach!" yelled Katie, as she hurtled towards Grandma's front door.

"Who cares, wasn't racing you anyway," was Will's quick response.

The next bit of fun was the doorbell; Grandma was hard of hearing so she had a special super loud bell which the kids loved to ring; as Katie got to the door first she got to ring the bell, much to her delight!

Will was acting as if he didn't care, but was planning to outdo Katie once they got inside the flat.

"Grandma!" the kids both bellowed as she opened the front door for them.

They felt really lucky to have such a wonderful Grandma as she gathered them into a great big warm, snugly hug. They were both thinking that Grandma had the best hugs of anyone, as she led them into her home.

"Off you go, you two, you know where everything is. I'm going to put the kettle on and make some tea, and what would you two like?" said Grandma.

Grandma always had lovely treats for the kids.

"Apple juice please," said Will.

"Could I have milkshake please?" said Katie, as she headed to the toy cupboard.

"Of course you can," said Grandma with a lovely big smile, adding, "oh it's so lovely to see you all."

Grandma had the best smile of anyone. It stretched right across her face and told you just how much she loved you, without even saying a word!

Turning away, Will quickly spotted one of his favourite things to play with, and it wasn't in the toy cupboard! It was Grandma's 'grabby thing'. Will didn't know what its proper name was, and he didn't really care; all the kids called it 'the grabby thing'. It had a handle and a long stick with grippers on the end. When you squeezed the handle, the grippers opened and then closed when you stopped squeezing; it was brilliant for picking up all sorts of things, and also brilliant for pinching annoying sisters who win races, even when you were not having a race!

Katie was already rooting through the toy cupboard.

Grandma was really good at finding different things for the kids to play with. She would look in all the charity shops near her flat for interesting games and toys, so there was nearly always something different to explore.

Then of course, there was the best fun of all, the marvellous, wonderful, magnificent rise and recline chair which Grandma sat in.

The kids had loads of fun taking it in turns to go up and down in the chair, pressing the buttons on the remote control, and Grandma never minded, even though it meant she had to sit on a hard chair; she would just sit and smile and shake her head in that particular way she had, thoroughly enjoying watching the kids enjoying themselves.

As well as a toy cupboard, there was a sweets and chocolate cupboard too; what more could a grandchild ask for!

"Help yourselves to some treats, you two," Grandma called from the kitchen. "Not too many treats though," added Mum quickly.

The kids hadn't really thought of Pearly since they had set off for Grandma's flat, and now they were merrily playing and munching on snacks, they didn't think of her at all or ponder on why she had become so elusive.

Life was definitely in a much happier place, and so the kids were just content to enjoy every moment.

Mum and Grandma were chatting whilst drinking tea and eating biscuits, and working on a big jigsaw puzzle together; Grandma always had a half completed jigsaw on her dining table, and everyone who visited added a few pieces to help complete the picture.

This was just another part of visiting Grandma that made it such good fun!

Katie was playing with a new friendship bracelet kit, but this was not going well at all! Beads seemed more inclined to fly across the carpet and roll under various chairs than fit smoothly and easily onto the bracelet string! She was feeling rather cross!

Will was sneaking quietly across the room in order to attack Katie with Grandma's 'grabby thing' when there was an almighty bang!

The kids both looked round at the same time to see poor Grandma lying on the floor, with Mum standing over her saying in a very worried voice, "Oh Mum, what happened, are you in pain? Oh dear, I hope this isn't serious!"

Mum had just popped into the kitchen to get more milk, Grandma had tried to stand too quickly and lost her balance!

The kids both had the same thought, *Where is Pearly? And, Can she help?*

As Mum was phoning for an ambulance, Will and Katie were trying to bring Pearly to the flat with the power of their thoughts. They were both desperately asking Pearly to help Grandma.

As Grandma was taken in the ambulance, Mum, Will and Katie followed in the car. They were all extremely worried, and the kids kept trying as hard as they could to summon Pearly.

For a second or two, they thought they got a glimpse of their gorgeous little Kitty Angel; for a moment or two, they thought they could feel her rumbling, soothing sound inside their heads; for a minute or two they were sure they could smell sweet flowers wafting around inside the car. Everything was so vague and insubstantial, they felt rather bewildered, and at the same time, very, very worried about their dear grandma!

As they arrived at the hospital, they saw Grandma vanishing into A&E.

Mum had a dreadful time finding somewhere to park, and was getting more and more flustered and angry as the minutes ticked away!

The kids just kept trying to get hold of the very elusive Pearly, feeling sure she would be able to help.

At last, they were parked and rushing into the hospital building.

The kids looked at each other, *Where is she, where is Pearly?* they were both thinking.

"Come on, you two," called Mum. "This way."

They followed a nurse along a narrow grey corridor that seemed to go on for miles!

"Here we are," said the nurse at last, as they were led into a cubicle to find Grandma sitting up smiling.

The doctor said that it was a miracle that nothing was broken; it was a miracle that there wasn't even bruising; it was a miracle that there was no pain!!!

Will and Katie looked at each other and both had the same thought, *'Our wonderful Kitty Angel, Pearly.'*

Grandma started to speak and so they all looked toward her lying on the bed.

"I've just had the most strange experience. I guess it's the shock of falling, but I swear I could smell gorgeous sweet flowers, I swear I could hear a strange, but lovely and soothing, rumbling sound in my head, and I swear I could see soft, downy white feathers floating down as I was wheeled along the corridor, but don't mind me. I'm just an old lady with silly ideas," she added, as the kids looked at each other and gave a knowing nod.

Grandma was allowed to go straight home, thankfully, and once they were absolutely, completely, and utterly sure she was fine, the family all headed back home.

They were hoping to find Pearly so that they could say a big thank you to her for taking care of their precious grandma.

They thought they caught a fleeting glimpse of something downy and white, but were unable to say for sure, as the image slipped from their sight almost as soon as they had seen it.

They were concerned about Pearly, and wondered what was happening to her, and why she seemed to be almost there but not quite!!!
Such a puzzle!
But on the other hand, they were equally relieved about their lovely grandma, and so happy that she was fine.

Chapter Eleven

The kids knew that Doods was back from his trip to the Outer Hebrides, as Nanny had phoned last night to ask if they could pop over after they had been to check on Grandma.

Mum was busy in the kitchen, humming to herself whilst getting the tea things ready, and the kids knew that there would definitely be cake on offer as Doods was coming to visit!

Will and Katie were very excited about seeing Nanny and Doods, and were really looking forward to hearing all about Doods' trip.

Their thoughts were so focused on the family gathering that they had little time to worry or ponder about their special, and rather elusive, Kitty Angel, Pearly.

In no time at all, there was a knock on the door.

The kids went dashing down the hallway to let Nanny and Doods in, shouting, "Nanny, Doods, we haven't seen you for ages," and enjoyed the big hugs they got from their lovely grandparents, who clearly both adored them!

Nanny was her usual smiling and chatty self, and had bought treats and snacks for everyone.

Nanny kept a bag in the boot of her car which she jokingly called 'The Nanny shop'. It was always full of treats and nice drinks for all the grandchildren.

Doods seemed a little subdued, but that wasn't too unusual; he was often quite serious and deep in thought, and the kids liked his calm, quiet ways.

Doods could always be relied on to deal with any family problem in an unflustered and measured manner, and when he was helping with homework and explaining something, he was so patient and encouraging; the kids thought the world of him!

Doods' trip to the Hebrides had been a huge success, many photos of birds had been taken, and Doods had been asked to enter several paintings in a Wildlife Art Exhibition.

The kids could see that Doods was excited, but at the same time a little worried; it was a big and important exhibition, and so there was a lot of pressure to get the paintings just right!

While they were enjoying their cake and drinks, Doods told Mum and the kids all about his trip.

How he had spotted an otter clambering over the rocks at the back of his cottage, and how he had seen white-tailed eagles soaring over the mountains at the front of his cottage; how he had seen red deer in the evenings and golden eagles almost every day.

The kids were fascinated and asked loads of questions until Mum said,

"Give Doods a break, you two, you'll wear him out with all your chattering."

"OK, Mum," said Will, looking a bit down in the mouth.

"OK, sorry," said Katie, looking a bit cross!

"It's just all so amazing!" they both chimed.

"Why don't you two go off and play for a bit while I have a chat with Nan and Doods?" continued Mum. "I've got lots to tell them," she added mysteriously!

The kids ran up to their room, and as they did so their thoughts went back to Pearly.

"Katie, what do you think has happened to Pearly?" said Will, feeling very perplexed.

"Search me," said Katie, feeling equally puzzled.

They pondered the Pearly situation for a while, wondering why she was only fleetingly in their lives now, and when they couldn't come up with any sensible answers, they decided to get down to some serious playing.

Mum, Nan and Doods had a really good catch up. They drank lots of tea and coffee, ate numerous slices of cake, and dunked rather a lot of chocolate biscuits!

Doods tried hard to focus on the family news but he was feeling rather distracted and troubled. He was delighted to see the kids and their mum but sadly couldn't quite shift a feeling of gloom hanging over him.

His thoughts kept returning to the up and coming art exhibition and he felt rather concerned, well more than concerned if he was honest; quite overwhelmed really! Rather than focusing on all his previous successes and all the praise he regularly got for his paintings, he couldn't summon up a positive thought, not one.

Doods could hear the kids playing upstairs, and thought to himself how lucky he was to have such a brilliant family, they really were a joy, and kept him going when the days seemed a little dark!

His thoughts were interrupted by Nanny, "Better be getting off now I think, before I eat any more cake," she said, laughing.

"So looking forward to seeing your paintings for the exhibition, Dad. Let me know when they're done and I'll pop over," said the kids' Mum.

She really loved her dad. He was always there when you needed advice or support; she could see that he was troubled but thought it best not to question him as sometimes that just made things worse. She would keep an eye on him and have a chat when the time felt right.

"Right kids, we're getting off now!" shouted Nanny up the stairs.

The kids came flying down from their room to give some big hugs to their lovely Nanny and Doods.

"See you both soon, I hope," said Doods after they'd had a lovely big hug each.

"Can I come over soon and see your photos, Doods?" said Will expectantly.

"Of course you can, Will," said Doods in response. "Any time you like, maybe after school one day," added Doods.

"Cool," said Will. "I'll text you in the week," he added.

Just as Nanny and Doods were leaving the house, Will and Katie heard Doods give a big sigh. They looked at each other with worried expressions.

"Poor Doods, he seems very troubled and down in the dumps," they both agreed. They thought of their lovely little Kitty Angel, Pearly. If she were around, they were sure that she would be able to help.

And they sent up a little prayer, hoping desperately that Pearly would hear them and help to lift the spirits of their dear Doods.

But where was she? they were both thinking.

What was she doing? they both wondered.

"We miss her so much," they both agreed.

At the same time though, life was feeling pretty good; Mum was happy and smiling most of the time, which was great because that meant they hardly got told off these days.

With these thoughts swilling around in their minds, they decided to go out to the local park for some mad fun on the climbing ropes and zip wire.

Chapter Twelve

Nanny and Doods made the short drive home, and whilst Nanny went swimming, Doods thought he would take the opportunity to look through his hundreds of photos and try to find some inspiration for his paintings. He only ever painted from his own photos; that was something he never wavered from.

After several hours of gazing at photos, but mainly gazing out of the window or just gazing into space, Doods decided to make some coffee and have a break. He just wasn't in the right frame of mind to make any proper judgement or choices about what to paint.

What am I to do? he thought to himself, as he ambled down to the kitchen and the lure of a good Americano from the coffee maker, with a biscuit or two of course! The day dragged on.

Nanny came back from swimming full of tales of the annoying women who swim up and down, chatting in a big group and just won't get out of the way and let others get past; so infuriating!!!

It was a bit of a distraction for Doods and made him smile briefly.

He felt worn out so decided on an early night; this meant about midnight for Doods, once he'd done the crossword, then the fiendish Sudoku, then the daily quiz and finally read several chapters of his favourite thriller!

He lay in bed tossing and turning restlessly, thinking he would never drop off, when suddenly it was morning!

He got up and did his morning stretches. He wasn't particularly into this Pilates stuff that Nanny liked to do, but the stretches helped to get him up and running in the mornings, rather than creaking about like some sad old fella.

He ambled downstairs to get his muesli sorted, and realised that he felt a little brighter and more positive.

Nanny was in the lounge already, which was most unusual as Nanny generally liked to lie in!

"Good morning," they both said at the same time, and burst out laughing.

"You look cheerful," said Nanny. "Did you have a good night?"

"Yes, I did actually, and I had a very, very strange dream," replied Doods.

"Oh really, what was it all about?" said Nanny.

"It's hard to explain," Doods answered, with a frown.

"Give it a go," said Nanny encouragingly.

"Well, OK, I'll try," said Doods.

"The dream didn't really start with any pictures, it was just as though I were standing in a flower garden, surrounded by all the most fragrant flowers in the world!" Doods began.

"The smell was gorgeous, so sweet, so fresh, and at the same time, so delicate!" he continued.

Nanny opened her eyes very wide and thought to herself, *Pearly? Could this really be something to do with that gorgeous Kitty Angel; mmmmm, I wonder.* Nanny said nothing, which was very unusual for her; she just waited for Doods to continue.

"It's most odd really," said Doods, "but next I seemed to feel a kind of bubbling feeling, no not bubbling, that isn't quite right, more a kind of rumbling inside my head; it was soothing and calming; quite lovely really!"

Nanny blinked hard and had to stop herself from blurting anything out about a Kitty Angel called Pearly, she knew that Doods would think she was completely bonkers if she as much as hinted at such a wonderful creature, so Nanny managed to stay quiet; which was actually very, very unusual for her!

Doods carried on with his description of the dream, unaware of Nanny's increasing excitement.

"The next thing I was aware of in this most unusual and rather lovely dream," Doods explained, "was the soft feeling of feathers falling against my skin; no not really feathers, more like fur; no that's not right either, oh dear how can I explain? I think the best way, the only way to put it is that I could feel something that was a mixture of feathers and fur; I know that sounds completely idiotic, as nothing like that actually exists, but that's the only way I can describe what I felt!" Nanny felt she was about to completely burst with the effort of saying nothing, it was much, much more than she could possibly manage, and so the words came flying out of her mouth:

"Pearly, the Kitty Angel!!!" she spluttered.

"What on earth are you blathering on about?" responded Doods. "Pearly, the Kitty Angel???" he repeated.

"The kids, it came to help the kids," Nanny blurted out.

"What! Are you completely mad!" was Doods' response, much as Nanny had expected.

"No, no, honestly, it's true," she explained.

"I've seen Pearly, she was with the kids, she was in their room, she's a Kitty Angel, it's true, really it is. She's got furry feathers and she 'rumbles' in your head, and there is a smell of flowers!!! And..."

Doods looked at Nanny as if she were speaking a foreign language; he raised his eyebrows, shrugged his shoulders, shook his head and just walked from the room muttering things about 'Angel madness!'

Oh bother, thought Nanny, *I knew that would be Doods' response, why did I have to open my silly mouth?*

And she wandered into the kitchen to make a soothing, calming cup of peppermint tea.

Meanwhile, Doods had escaped to the peace and quiet of his study to gaze at photos, and begin another day of attempting to prepare for the looming art exhibition.

"Kitty Angel!" he muttered under his breath, as he shook his head, and started to gather up his art materials.

Ah well, better make a start I guess, Doods thought to himself, as he started to look at his collection of photos online.

After browsing through the first few pictures, he was inspired by an unusual shot of a Robin, it was looking straight at the camera with a cute and cheeky expression; 'Don't remember seeing that one before!' Doods pondered.

He quickly got his pencils, paints, brushes and water ready, and began sketching out the initial outlines.

Suddenly, it was lunchtime; Nanny was calling up the stairs that there was a hot bacon roll waiting downstairs for Doods.

Wow, lunch time already, Doods thought to himself. *It just seems like minutes since I started sketching!*

Suddenly, he realised he was really hungry, and the thought of a bacon roll made him bound down the stairs.

Nanny was delighted to see Doods looking so bright.

"Picture going well?" she dared to ask.

"Not too bad," was Doods' modest reply.

Doods was always extremely modest about his art; everyone else would say it was 'wonderful', 'marvellous' or 'brilliant', but Doods would just say "It's not bad", "It's OK", or "I'm reasonably happy with it"; he was a real perfectionist.

Doods went straight back to the study after his rather tasty bacon roll, followed by some strawberries and a cereal bar, and of course an Americano coffee.

The afternoon went quickly and soon the painting was complete.

Doods had received a text from Will during the afternoon asking if it was OK for him to pop over after school one day. Doods naturally said 'Yes', he was always more than happy to see the grandchildren; they always lifted his spirits. Will was also very keen on wildlife, so they always had lots to chat about.

There was an atmosphere of calm throughout the evening, and Nanny was delighted, although she didn't dare mention anything about Angels, Kitty or otherwise, but she was sure that there was some 'Kitty Angel' magic at work here. She couldn't wait to tell the kids!

That night, Doods slept soundly and the following morning he was bright as a button again; Nanny didn't ask about his dreams, but felt sure that his night would have been filled with beautiful flowery scents, calm, soothing rumbling sounds, and the soft touch of furry feathers.

After his usual breakfast of muesli, banana and an Americano, Doods was straight up to his study; he was on a roll and didn't want to break the rhythm.

Looking through his photos, Doods soon spotted a perfect shot of a Grey Heron, *That's the one for today's painting,* he thought to himself with a smile and soon got busy with pencils, brushes and paint.

The day whizzed by, and with Nanny supplying more bacon rolls, biscuits and coffee, the painting was completed in record time.

The evening was once more calm and peaceful, and Nanny was again sure that this was the 'Kitty Angel' effect.

She was picking the kids up from school tomorrow, and couldn't wait to tell them; she just knew they would be thrilled to bits.

The next day dawned bright and breezy.

Doods was bright and breezy too after another lovely night of flowery scent, feathery fur and rumbling relaxation.

He bounded up the stairs to his study, more than ready for another day of drawing and painting; as he got up to the landing, Nanny called up to him,

"I'm off to my aquarobics class now, then I'll swim a few lengths and probably meet up with friends for a cuppa afterwards; oh and don't forget, I'm picking Will and Katie up today!"

Oh, where on Earth does she get all that energy from! Doods thought to himself with a smile.

Doods was soon concentrating on his next painting, a brilliant blue and orange Kingfisher perched on a gnarled old branch; "It would make a perfect contrast to the Robin and the Heron', he muttered to himself."

He couldn't quite get to grips with the fact that the paintings were all suddenly going so well for him, but he was extremely delighted with the way they were turning out.

Nothing to do with 'Angels', Kitty Angels, or any of that silly nonsense, Doods was thinking, as he mixed up the colours for his painting.

Doods was also thinking about his grandchildren as he sorted through his paint tubes. He really was blessed to have such a great family. He knew Will was planning to pop round later in the week, and that was really something to look forward to.

Of course Doods had no idea that the kids had been sending up a prayer asking the very gorgeous Pearly to help him.

As far as Doods was concerned, any talk of anything 'Angel' related was nothing but utter balderdash, and that was all there was to it!

Chapter Thirteen

Nanny was just heading out of the sports centre after having had a really good work out.

Aquarobics had been brilliant, it was such good fun jumping about in the water, splashing everyone, with all that great music blasting out; the 30 lengths afterwards had been a bit of a struggle, but a nice cup of tea is just what I need now, thought Nanny.

Nanny started thinking about Doods as she headed to the cafe to meet up with some friends.

It's brilliant that Pearly has been helping Doods with his artwork, particularly as he thinks it's all a load of nonsense! I wish he could believe in our lovely little Kitty Angel, then maybe he would catch a glimpse of her, thought Nanny.

After a cup of tea, and a nice slice of chocolate cake, and an even nicer long chat with her friends, Nanny felt very relaxed and started to think about all the things she needed to do before she collected the kids.

The day went quickly and soon it was time to pick Will and Katie up from school. Nanny couldn't wait to see the two of them, and was bursting to tell them about Doods and Kitty Angel.

She was standing outside the school gates when the kids came racing through the crowd of Mums, Nans, Granddads, and other assorted relatives and children, all heading in the same direction!

"Hi, you two!" Nanny called.

"Nanny!" the kids both shrieked at the top of their voices; as they bounded towards her, their bags flying out behind them.

"Heigh, steady on you two," Nanny said as she gave them both a great big hug. They quickly walked over to the car, or rather, Nanny walked whilst Will and

Katie ran as fast as they could, trying to get to the car first and be the 'winner'!

"Check out the Nanny Shop, you two," said Nanny as she started opening the boot of the car.

"Great! Thanks, Nanny," said Will, as he rummaged through the contents looking for his favourite bar and drink.

"Thanks a lot, Nanny," said Katie as she tried to push Will out of the way and get first choice!

"There's plenty for both of you," Nanny said, smiling to herself.

"Anyone would think you two hadn't eaten for months," she said, laughing, as she went round the car to the driver's side.

"I've got something great to tell you two, it's about Doods and Pearly," Nanny told the children.

"Doods and Pearly!" the kids both shrieked!

"What has happened?" asked Katie, looking puzzled.

"Doods and Pearly, no way!' said Will, laughing his head off.

As they were driving back to the kids' house, Nanny told Will and Katie all about Doods and his dreams, and the lovely calm atmosphere at home, and the successful paintings.

The kids were thrilled.

So, Pearly was still with them, even if they rarely got a glimpse of her these days, they both thought.

All was going well for the kids too. They hardly ever got told off these days, and Mum was smiling and humming nearly every evening when she got home from work; the only thing they still thought about, apart from their darling Pearly, of course; was the longed for, white, fluffy, little kitten!

Will and Katie had a good time after school with Nanny.

The three of them chatted a lot about the Pearly situation, but could come to no conclusion; so eventually the kids just put it out of their minds and focused instead on winding each other up, which was great fun!

Later that evening, Will made his plan to call on Doods after school the next day. He was really looking forward to seeing Doods, they always had such great chats about anything to do with wildlife; maybe they would plan a walking day out together too, that would be brilliant!

Chapter Fourteen

The next morning when the kids woke up, there was a faint but glorious smell of flowers in their room.

Strange, we haven't had that lovely smell of flowers floating around the house since Pearly arrived, thought Will, feeling a little excited.

Katie took a deep breath in as she woke up and muttered sleepily:

"Mmmm, nice smell." She didn't really register the significance as she was barely awake.

"Breakfast's nearly ready, you two," Mum called up the stairs.

The kids were so busy getting ready that thoughts about the lovely smell of flowers vanished from their minds.

They were enjoying their chocolate brioche and milk shakes, which were a real treat for mid-week.

Mum must be in a very good mood today, they both thought.

At which point, Mum took a sniff and said, "Katie, have you been pinching my body spray?"

"No, Mum, I wouldn't help myself to your spray, you know I always ask first."

"I wonder what that lovely smell is then, can you two smell flowers in here, or is it me?" said Mum.

The kids both looked at each other and shrugged their shoulders.

Mum said she would be going out at the weekend and so Nanny and Doods would be coming over to babysit.

They were all feeling really happy about how Doods was getting on with his paintings; they were all finished now and ready for the exhibition, brilliant!

Nanny and Doods had been really sorry that they hadn't been able to get to Will's concert earlier in the term, and said that they would make it up to him in some way. He wondered what his treat might be.

Luckily, a DVD had been made of the whole evening so they would be able to see Wills' performance when they came round.

Mum still seemed really happy, and hummed a tune as she made their packed lunches.

School went quickly and occasionally both Will and Katie thought they caught a glimpse of Kitty Angel, but again it was as if a little shadow passed by that was filmy and insubstantial, most puzzling.

There was no Kitty Angel in their room when they got home.

The rest of the week was much the same:

Mum smiling and humming.

A haunting scent of flowers that seemed to be getting fainter day by day.

Homework to do.

Arguments to have with each other, but not too many!

And that sense of a filmy Kitty Angel that wasn't quite there.

As the weekend got closer, Katie started to fret a little about the up and coming gymnastics trials. She had a couple more weeks before the date but felt her confidence slipping away. She had her regular class on Saturday mornings, and knew that this particular weekend the team coach would be choosing who would represent the club as part of the squad.

Katie knew that her flexibility meant she was good on the floor exercises; she knew the parallel bars would be a challenge, but as for the beam and the horse she was similar to the other girls in her group.

Anything could happen on Saturday!

She thought of Kitty Angel, as she stroked her good luck fluffy unicorn toy, and wished that she was here to comfort her and make everything alright.

There was a sense that she was, and yet wasn't, still part of their lives. It was perplexing, but at the same time not too distressing!

Suddenly, the weekend was upon her!

She woke up with butterflies in her stomach and looked around for any signs of Pearly.

Was that a very faint smell of flowers she could detect, or was it just her imagination? There was no Kitty Angel to be seen, of that she was sure.

Oh well, thought Katie, *I'd better get up and start getting myself sorted out for gym club.*

But in the back of her mind was a sadness at not seeing Pearly when she opened her eyes this morning, a feeling that in some way she had been let down.

"Come on, Katie!" shouted Mum up the stairs. "We don't want to be late," she added.

Katie looked through her leotards, most of which were in a pile on the floor, alongside her leggings and hoodie. She always intended to put them in her drawer but somehow never got round to doing the job!

Which one shall I choose? she thought to herself. *The blue with gold pattern or the purple and silver? Oh I just can't make up my mind!*

Then peeping out from the bottom of the pile she spotted a package.

"What can that be?" she puzzled.

Grabbing the parcel, she suddenly remembered; feeling excited and really dreadful at the same time, as it all came back to her that Nanny had promised to order her something new for gymnastics. She remembered now that a parcel had arrived but she'd been dashing out for a sleepover and just dropped it on her bedroom floor and forgot!

How ghastly, how vile, how ungrateful of me, Katie thought.

She ripped the paper off, then the bubble wrap and finally the plastic packet, and there it was, the most beautiful leotard she had ever seen. It was gorgeous, with a pale mauve and sky blue design on a shiny Lycra leotard that glowed in a magical and entrancing way.

Katie thought she detected a faint flowery smell emanating from the package but pushed that thought to the back of her mind in her haste to try on the fabulous gift.

Perfect, Katie thought as she pulled it on.

She hastily sent a text to Nanny to say a BIG thank you for her gift, and then ran downstairs to show Will and Mummy.

Mummy was putting out breakfast, and was cheerful and smiling.

Will was busy finishing off some sketches of cars that he had been working on. They both looked up as Katie came dashing into the room.

"Wow!" said Will, which was high praise indeed from a big brother.

Mummy said, "Oh my gosh!"

They both agreed that Katie looked amazing; her confidence soared and she felt ready for anything.

Katie decided to head down to the basement before eating breakfast and do a warm up and some basic stretches. She then thought she would run through her mat routine to fix it in her mind.

As the music played from her iPod, she went into a world of her own; spinning, tumbling and cartwheeling through her routine. It was wonderful, it was what she really loved to do, she felt alive and as if she was part of the music as it flowed around the room.

She had just finished the final tumbling sequence when Mummy called down to say breakfast was on the table.

Katie suddenly realised that she was starving, so happily ran up the stairs to join Mummy and Will for breakfast.

Breakfast was yummy chocolate brioche and berries as a treat.

The kids both wolfed them down, and now it was time for Katie to go to gym. Will was going cycling that morning with a friend, so he set off as Katie and Mummy headed for gym club.

"Now, don't be too disappointed if you don't get picked for the squad," Mummy said to Katie, as they pulled into the car park at the gym.

"There's a lot of tough competition for the few places," she added.

As she said these words, she was wishing with all her heart that Katie would be successful; she knew how much the competition meant to her.

"It's fine, Mum," Katie said in reply, although inside she was not feeling so flippant. The competition was what she had been working towards and she would be crushed, gutted and really, really fed up if she wasn't chosen.

Where was Pearly? Katie thought.

I really need her today.

She thought she saw a flash of something white and fluffy from the corner of her eye, but when she looked round, there was nothing to be seen.

She did feel very calm though, and confident. She smiled to herself and felt the morning was going to go well.

Meanwhile, Mummy was still humming to herself and had a happy smile on her face.

The gym session was going well.

Everyone was performing to a high standard as they all wanted to be chosen for the squad.

Katie felt she was doing well. Her floor work, she knew, would be the clincher, as it was her best element.

When she finished the final tumbling sequence, she was sure she had done enough to be chosen, and waited in anticipation for the team coach to make the choices for the squad.

The choosing seemed to take for ever, and all her best friends had been picked. Katie was just beginning to think she hadn't quite done enough to make the grade when there was a lovely waft of flowery scent, and a feeling of furry feathers rubbing up against her arm, at which point she heard the coach call her name and realised that she had been chosen too!

She was thrilled, over the moon, ecstatic!

As she calmed down, Katie began to ponder about whether 'Kitty Angel' had actually been there with her at the gym, or had she imagined it?

She hadn't actually seen Pearly, but she was sure she had felt her nuzzling up against her arm, and there was that lovely, flowery smell; what a puzzle!

Anyway, the morning had been a great success and she was going to be part of the gym squad representing her club, fantastic!

Mum was thrilled when she picked Katie up, and still in a great mood.

They went and collected Will, and all had ice cream together to celebrate.

Chapter Fifteen

That night, Nanny and Doods were coming over to babysit while Mummy went out for the evening.

Mummy was really bright and bubbly as she got ready for the evening and when Nanny and Doods arrived, Katie couldn't wait to tell them about her success at Gym club. They were thrilled for her and said they would definitely be coming to the competition to watch her perform.

Both Will and Katie couldn't help but think that life had been very good since Kitty Angel had arrived in their bedroom.

They couldn't quite understand why they didn't really, properly see her anymore. Part of them felt sad, but part of them couldn't help but feel happy about how life was for all of them at the moment, including Mummy.

They had a great evening with Nanny and Doods and soon it was time for bed. The two of them tripped up the stairs chatting and bundled into the bedroom without really looking, when to their enormous surprise, there was Pearly, their adorable Kitty Angel sitting in the middle of Katie's bed.

"Where have you been?" both the children shouted together!

"I've really missed you!" blurted Katie.

"I've missed you too!" muttered Will.

Pearly looked up at them both with her enormous blue eyes and began to explain, "My job is done, and so I can't stay any longer. The gap between our worlds is opening up, and once I'm getting close to leaving, my physical body finds it much more difficult to appear."

"So that's why we kept smelling the flowers but couldn't see you!" Katie said.

"And that's why we kept feeling you were around even though you weren't, if you get what I mean?" uttered Will.

"That's right," Pearly confirmed.

"I kept trying to show myself but once my time to go is near, it gets harder and harder!"

"But we can see you now," spluttered Will.

"Yes, we can see you clearly now, why's that?" Katie asked in puzzlement.

"It's just the way it works on my final visit," Pearly replied.

"Final visit?" the children both spluttered.

"Noooooo!" they cried in unison.

"I have no choice," Pearly said quietly.

"I've done what was needed," she explained.

"The final part will become clear later tonight; I'll always be looking down at you and helping gently from afar, but now I have to go."

And as Pearly slowly vanished from sight, the children heard her gently calling to them, saying,

"Look after each other, believe in yourselves, strive to be happy and stay strong."

And with these final words Pearly, the beautiful Kitty Angel, vanished from sight. The children were shocked and sad, but at the same time they were grateful and honoured that Pearly had come into their life, a life that had gotten better and better, and in which they had felt happier and stronger over the last few months. They wondered what Pearly had meant about the final part?

They were puzzling this out when they heard the front door open and could just make out Nanny and Doods talking to Mummy, and then the sound of another voice, a man's voice.

They crept out of their room and peered over the banister, they could just make out the shape of a man, he had his arm round Mummy's shoulder and Mummy was smiling broadly.

At this point, she looked up, and laughingly shouted,

"Come on down you two, there's someone here who would really like to see you both..."

"Well, I should say someone and 'something'," she added quickly.

The kids both started to run down the stairs.

As they got about halfway, they thought they could hear a faint scratching sound.

Mmmmmmm, they both thought, feeling a little puzzled.

Then as they got a bit nearer to the hallway, they were sure they heard a faint mewing sound.

Ahhhhhhhhhh, they both thought, feeling rather excited!

When they arrived in the hallway, they saw clearly that there was a little box next to Mummy, and that box had 'Pets-for-all' printed on it.

As Mummy bent down to open the box, the kids could hardly contain their excitement, and they thought they would burst with happiness when peeping out of the box was the cutest, cuddliest, furriest, softest little white kitten; so perfect with a little pink nose and beautiful blue eyes.

Will and Katie looked at each other with big grins on their faces and both at the same time said,

"Pearly, that's what we'll call her."

And as they picked the little white kitten up and started to cuddle and stroke her, they became aware that there was a faint smell of flowers drifting around them, and they knew then for certain that their very own special little Kitty Angel would never be too far away.

From then on, they became a very happy family of four, or should that be five! Life was still full of the usual ups and downs of family life, but the good days far outnumbered the bad ones.

Their little white, fluffy kitten, Pearly, grew into a beautiful, loving cat, bringing hours and hours of cuddles and fun.

The kids never forgot Kitty Angel, and they would sometimes speak quietly with Nanny about this amazing time.

They remembered Pearly's beautiful big blue eyes and the way she seemed to get right inside their heads with a delightful, tickling kind of rumbling.

They thought about how Pearly managed to make everything feel calm and peaceful, and what a wonderful and truly special experience they had lived through, one that they would never, ever forget!

The End